I KNOW A SURPRISE

BY DOROTHY WALTER BARUCH

Author of *Big Fellow*

Nancy is a little girl just about your age, or maybe she is not as old as you. She has some of the nicest pets at her home. There is a kitten and there is a dog and there is a rabbit and there is a chicken. Maybe you have pets of this kind too. Nancy has still another pet. You would never guess what it is, for you probably do not have a pet like this one. It is a tortoise. Have you ever seen a tortoise?

One day Nancy went all around the house and the yard singing a little song, which went like this:

> I know a surprise
> I know a surprise
> I know,
> > I know
> > A surprise.

She sang this song to the cat, she sang it to the dog, she sang it to the rabbit and the chicken and the tortoise. And every one of them began to follow Nancy because they wanted to know what this wonderful surprise could be.

Now of course you will want to know, too, for it really was the nicest surprise in all the world.

* *

I KNOW A SURPRISE

by
Dorothy Walter Baruch
PICTURES BY
George and Doris Hauman

This special edition is published by arrangement with the publisher
of the regular edition, Lothrop, Lee & Shepard Company, Boston

CADMUS BOOKS

E. M. HALE AND COMPANY
EAU CLAIRE, WISCONSIN

I KNOW A SURPRISE

I KNOW A SURPRISE, I KNOW A SURPRISE.

I KNOW, I KNOW, A SURPRISE.

Music by
DOROTHY VAN DEMAN

"I know a surprise,
I know a surprise,
I know,
   I know
      A surprise," sang Nancy.

SHE ran to tell her cat.

"I know something you don't know," Nancy said
to her cat. "It's a surprise."

The cat went, "Miew" and "Miaow." The cat
purred, "Zrrr," softly.

Then Nancy laughed. "Kitty, I'll take you to see it."

So Nancy picked up the cat and carried him into the house — right into the living room. And there Nancy put the cat *down*.

Then she smiled mysteriously at the cat.

Then she shook her finger at the cat.

And she said, " Sh. Don't you make any noise. Just wait here till I come back. And then I'll take you to see the surprise."

"I know a surprise,
I know a surprise,
  I know,
    I know
      A surprise," sang Nancy.

SHE ran to tell her dog.

She lifted up his long, floppy ear. She bent down and whispered into it, "I know something you don't know. It's a surprise."

The dog went, "Bow wow." The dog went, "Ark, ark." "Bow wow" and "Ark, ark."

Then Nancy laughed. " Doggie, I'll take you to see it."

So Nancy picked up the dog and carried him into the house — right into the dining room. And there Nancy put the dog *down*.

Then she smiled mysteriously at the dog.

Then she shook her finger at the dog.

And she said, " Sh. Don't you make any noise. Just wait here till I come back. And then I'll take *you* to see the surprise."

> "I know a surprise,
> I know a surprise,
> I know,
>   I know
>   A surprise," sang Nancy.

SHE ran to tell her rabbit.

"I know something you don't know," Nancy said to her rabbit. "It's a surprise."

The rabbit wiggled his nose. The rabbit flipped an

ear. The rabbit wiped his whiskers with his two paws.

So Nancy picked up the rabbit and carried him into the house — right into the kitchen. And there Nancy put the rabbit *down*.

Then she smiled mysteriously at the rabbit.

Then she shook her finger at him.

And she said, " Sh. Don't you make any noise. Just wait here till I come back. And then I'll take *you* to see the surprise."

I know a surprise,
I know a surprise,
I know,
I know
A surprise," sang Nancy.

SHE ran to tell her chicken.

"I know something you don't know," Nancy said to her chicken. "It's a surprise."

The chicken stretched her neck. The chicken went, "Cuck cuck caw-awk, cuck cuck caw-awk." The chicken

scratched around on the ground — scritch, scritch scratch.

So Nancy picked up the chicken and carried her into the house — right into the bathroom. And there Nancy put the chicken *down*.

Then she smiled mysteriously at the chicken.

Then she shook her finger at her.

And she said, " Sh. Don't you make any noise. Just wait here till I come back. And then I'll take *you* to see the surprise."

         "I know a surprise,
         I know a surprise,
         I know,
           I know
            A surprise," sang Nancy.

SHE ran to tell her tortoise.

"I know something you don't know," Nancy said to her tortoise. "It's a surprise."

She bent down and touched the tortoise's hard shell back.

The tortoise pulled in its head, right into its shell.   And it pulled in its feet.   And it pulled in its tail.

So Nancy picked up the tortoise and carried it into the house — right into her bedroom.   And there Nancy put the tortoise *down*.

Then she smiled mysteriously at the tortoise.

Then she shook her finger at the tortoise.

And she said, " Sh.   Don't you make any noise.   Just wait till I come back.   And then I'll take *you* to see the surprise."

"I know a surprise,
    I know a surprise,
    I know,
        I know
            A surprise," sang Nancy.

SHE went to tell her doll about it.

"I know something you don't know," Nancy said to

her doll. "It's a surprise."

The doll's smile looked as though the doll were pleased.
So Nancy took her up in her arms.

"Come, dolly," she said. "We're ready now to get
the others. Then we'll *all* go together to see the surprise."

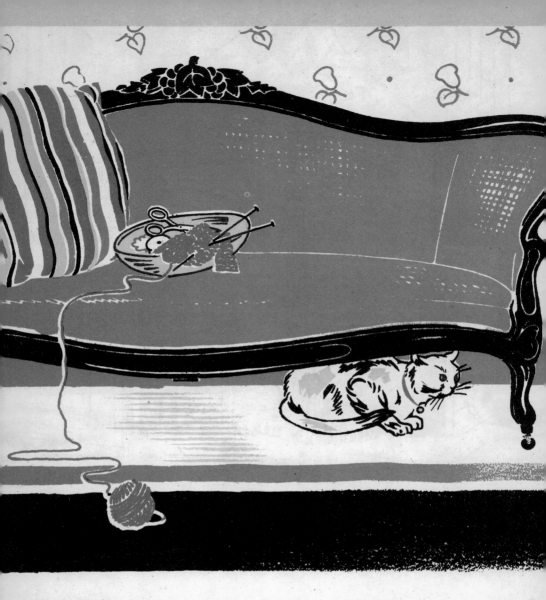

"FIRST we'll get kitty."

So Nancy went to the living room. She looked all around the living room. But she did not see kitty.

She looked this way. She looked that way. But she did not see kitty.

And then, all of a sudden, she saw him. He was under the sofa.

He went, " Miew " and " Miaow."

" Come, kitty," called Nancy. " Come along with dolly. Come along with me. We're going to see the surprise."

"Now we'll get doggie."

So Nancy went to the dining room. But she did not see her dog.

She looked this way. She looked that way. But she did not see her dog.

And then, all of a sudden, she saw him. He was under

the table.

He went, " Bow wow " and " Ark, ark." " Bow wow " and " Ark, ark."

" Come along, doggie," called Nancy. " Come along with dolly, and with kitty, and with me. We're going to see the surprise."

"Now we'll get bunny."

So Nancy went to the kitchen. But she did not see her bunny.

She looked this way. She looked that way. But she did not see her bunny.

And then, all of a sudden, she saw him. He was under the stove.

"Come, bunny," called Nancy. "Come along with dolly, and with kitty, and with doggie, and with me. We're going to see the surprise."

"NOW we'll get the chicken."

So Nancy went to the bathroom. She looked all around the bathroom. But she did not see her chicken.

She looked this way. She looked that way. But she did not see her chicken.

And then, all of a sudden, Nancy saw her. She was
behind the bathtub.

She went, " Cuck cuck caw-awk, cuck cuck caw-awk."

" Come, chickie," called Nancy. " Come along with
dolly, and with doggie, and with kitty, and with bunny,
and with me. We're going to see the surprise."

"Now we'll get the tortoise."
So Nancy went to her bedroom. She looked all around
her bedroom. But she did not   see   her   tortoise.
And then, all of a sudden, she saw it. It was under

the big green chair.

"Come, tortoise," called Nancy. "Come along with dolly, and with doggie, and with kitty, and with bunny, and with chicken, and with me. We're going to see the surprise."

So they all started out to see the surprise.
First went Nancy, carrying her doll.
And then came her cat.
And then came her dog.

And then came her rabbit.
And then came her chicken.
And then, at the very end, came her tortoise.
They all followed Nancy.

NANCY came to some steps.
Up, up, up the steps she went.
And· they all followed her.

Nancy came to a hall.
Walk, walk, walk, along the hall she went.
And they all followed her.

NANCY came to a door.

"No," said Nancy, "that's not the *right* door. The surprise is *not* in there."

Nancy came to another door.

"No," said Nancy, "*that's* not the right door. The surprise is not in there."

Nancy came to still another door.

"Sh," said Nancy. "This *is* the right door. The surprise *is* in here."

And Nancy put her hand on the door knob, and she turned it very slowly.

And Nancy *pushed* the door, and she pushed it open all the way.

" HERE'S the surprise," cried Nancy.

And there? . . . Yes, there, in front of them, was a tiny little bed. It was covered with a pink cover.

And in the bed lay Nancy's brand-new *baby brother*.

" Isn't he a grand surprise? "

Mother was in the room, too.

" My goodness gracious! " said mother, when she saw

all the animals in the doorway. And she held up her
hands.

Nurse was in the room, too.

"Oh me oh my, oh me oh my!" cried nurse. And
she shook her head.

Daddy was in the room, too.

"Well — well I never!" he grinned.

And then he began to laugh.

DADDY laughed and laughed — a big deep laugh,
"Ho — ho — ho — ho!"

So mother had to begin to laugh, too.

Mother laughed and laughed — a fast, little
up-and-down laugh, "Ha — ah — ah — ah — hah."

So nurse had to begin to laugh, too.

Nurse laughed and laughed — a sharp, high-up laugh,
"Heeeee — ee."

So Nancy had to begin to laugh, too.

They *all* laughed and laughed.

All of them laughed but baby brother. He just lay in his tiny little bed covered with a pink cover.

And *he* slept and slept.

He did not seem to know at all that Nancy had brought her doll and all her animal friends to see *him* as a surprise.